Tales from the Canyons of the Damned

PRESENTED BY USA TODAY BESTSELLING AUTHOR
DANIEL ARTHUR SMITH

Tales from the Canyons of the Damned 30

All rights reserved Holt Smith ltd

Collection Copyright © 2019 by Daniel Arthur Smith

Something Bad by Jeremy Essex. Copyright © 2018 Jeremy Essex. Used by permission of the author.

On a Front Porch on a November Afternoon by M. Regan. Copyright © 2018 M. Regan. Used by permission of the author.

The End of the World and a Super 88 by Michael Ezell. Copyright © 2018 Michael Ezell. Used by permission of the author.

Winning in Real Estate by Lara Frater. Copyright © 2018 Lara Frater. Used by permission of the author.

The Lost Tapes—Shane Starr by Daniel Arthur Smith. Copyright © 2018 Daniel Arthur Smith. Used by permission of the author.

First Edition

Special thanks to editor Jessica West

ISBN: 978-1-946777-79-9

Cover By Daniel Arthur Smith

Horror Fiction from Holt Smith ltd
Agroland
Tower
Attack of the Kung Fu Mummies

For Susan, Tristan, & Oliver, as all things are.
&
A Special Thank You To
Shay VanZwoll, Dan Brown, & Kevin G. Summers for
their readership & continued support.

Something Bad

Jeremy Essex

IT HAPPENED AT FOUR FIFTEEN in the afternoon on Monday the fourth of May, just as the last cargo train of the day shuddered past the windows of the Thorton's Freight building. Maureen Collins looked up from her desk, feeling for a moment as if she was waking from a dream.

What was that? she thought dazedly. *What... what just happened?*

She looked around her partitioned office, convinced there was something out of place. There was the familiar pattern of her filing cabinets, the line of dusty trophies arranged along the top, the vertical blinds hanging like giant dangling insects above the window shelf. Just her comfy, familiar office. Everything as it always was.

But why wouldn't it be? she thought. *Why do I feel so strange?*

She rubbed her thighs. She'd been sitting here too long, trying to get these damn accounts finished. Her brain needed another caffeine boost. Picking up her cup, Maureen strode out into the main office.

"Steve?" she called out to her chief accounts assistant. "Have you got those..."

Her words froze in her mouth. Six banks of unoccupied desks lined the utterly deserted office. The empty surfaces reached backwards to the fire door at the rear of the floor. Her distorted reflection stared back at her from the small, frosted glass windows.

She looked at her watch.

It was quarter past four.

She looked up again, as if expecting to find that her eyes had somehow deceived her.

There was nobody here.

But just a few moments ago, *everybody* had been out here. She had seen them. She had heard them. Just before the...

Before the train came past...

Something touched her mind, like the memory of a dark, forgotten dream. She suddenly turned and walked across to the windows.

I can't have missed the fire alarm, she thought. *Did I fall asleep? Is that what happened just now? Am I so tired that I actually fell asleep? Just for a second?*

The road below her was deserted. No crowd of people lined up outside the building. Not one solitary person walked along the stretch of pavement sloping down to the Sainsbury's on the corner. Not a single car was visible on the road.

Baffled, Maureen wandered through the office doors into the outer hallway. Standing at the top of the shadow covered stairs, she listened for the tell-tale sounds of people on the other floors. A ghostly moan filled the hallway as the wind whipped around the building's outer walls, the toilet doors drifting open by themselves as if pushed by phantom hands. Maureen felt as if she was standing in a dream.

A dream.

Something tugged at her mind.

Is that what had made her feel so strange just now? The memory of a dream? A glimpse of some forgotten nightmare, like a giant, monstrous eye flickering open in the pitch darkness of her subconscious?

I remembered a dream.

And then the train came past.

The train.

She ran her hands down her face.

What happened? Just now...something happened.

A violent chill seized her body.

Something bad.

Darkness flickered in her mind again. She turned and took a slow, trembling step towards the window by the lift doors.

Out there.

I saw something, out there.

Four floors down below, a mass of shivering trees covered the steep embankment sloping down to the black, gaping mouth of the railway tunnel on the edge of the industrial estate. Steel railings bordered the embankment on either side. As she looked down at the thrashing leaves, a shadow seemed to stride out of the tunnel, forcing its way through the trees.

The toilet door banged, the heavy draft actually pulling at the hem of Maureen's skirt. When she looked back down, she saw nothing but the waving trees.

He came... a voice seemed to say. *He came... out of the dark...*

She closed her eyes. What in the name of bloody hell was wrong with her? If everybody was gone from her floor then they must have been summoned to one of the others floors for some kind of announcement. She'd been so wrapped up in what she was doing that she just hadn't noticed everyone filing past her window.

There, she told herself. That was the explanation. What on earth had made her have a panic attack like that? Thank god no one else had seen her. This was not fitting behavior for the head of accounts.

Her heels clattered loudly as she hurried down the staircase, her heart still pounding in her chest. No wonder she was in such a bloody state! She'd been working too damned hard. She'd been here until ten o'clock every night this week and she knew she would be here late tonight as well.

Bill was going to be annoyed.

You said you'd be home on time, she heard his voice in her mind. *Bloody hell, Maureen, you don't think of anything but that damn job.*

Her own phantom voice responded. *Do you know how difficult it is for a woman to get to the top, Bill?*

Of course, I do. It's just that I never see you. The children never see you.

I have to work, Bill.

The long silence filled her memory.

I understand, Bill finally said. *I understand that you have to prove yourself. I just hope, Maureen, that you don't regret the sacrifices you make.*

Maureen smiled as she stepped off the staircase. Bill was such a wonderful man. She'd done the right thing in marrying him.

Bill.

A cold hand suddenly touched her. Had the dream been about Bill? Was that the memory that she'd felt just now? In her darkest dreams, had he somehow been taken from her, leaving her cold and alone, with no one with whom to share her life?

God. How could something so disturbing be in her soul?

She hurried through the doorway into the third-floor office. The doors clattered behind her, echoing through the deserted floor. The standing figures of the filing cabinets were the only occupants of the silent room. The desks were dusty and bare, as if they hadn't been used for months.

But just half an hour ago, there had been twenty people down here. She had seen them with her own eyes. When she'd gone to talk to Don on the transport desk, she'd had to shout over the cacophony of swearing voices and ringing phones. She been talking to Don, and...

Something happened to her thoughts.

Wait a minute. Hadn't that been yesterday?

She looked around the office, catching sight of the railway track outside. Again, the memory of watching the cargo train flickered in her mind.

She'd been down here. She was sure that she had. Then she had gone back upstairs and returned to her desk. She had been very tired, but she had forced herself to keep working on the Chrysler accounts, knowing that they had to be finished by five o'clock today. She'd been turning the figures over in her mind, then something had distracted her. She'd turned to the window and seen...

Something.

Something out there.

The train charging past on the track.

I saw the train...

5

And it made me remember... something...
Something...

She tried to grasp it. The flash of a dream. Her hand reaching out to Bill, desperately trying to touch him... reaching out to the dark figure before her.

Horror suddenly filled her soul. She stared at the deserted, unused, ancient office. No one had used this place for months, or even years. She stumbled forwards, her high heeled shoes catching on the carpet. This wasn't real! She knew it wasn't real! She was going to get out of here. She was going to see her husband again. She was going to be happy, and do all the things she'd always wanted to do. She still had time.

She still had *time!*

She raced through the doorway and down the staircase, her hand touching the dust covered bannister. On the ground floor, she tried to open the front door that would allow her outside into the car park, out into the real world where her husband was waiting for her. She shook the sturdy glass door, but it wouldn't budge. It was firmly locked.

Locked? Why would it be locked at...

She looked at her watch and saw that it was precisely four fifteen.

Four fifteen?

The hands of her watch were frozen at the same time as when she had looked at them a few minutes ago. Just after...

It happened.

She backed away from the door, her hands trembling against her face.

"No!" she screamed. "Please! *No! Don't let it be real!*"

She fell against the stairs.

It happened at four fifteen.

That was the story everyone told. The story whispered from mouth to mouth by the people who passed through the building.

The woman was working here all by herself. It was a bank holiday, and everybody else was at home. But the woman was always here. Weekends, holidays, she was always working.

They say the man hid in the railway tunnel. He'd already killed a young girl in Colchester, but the police weren't looking for him out here. He'd hidden in the tunnel until he was sure there was no one else in the building. Then he came out and crept through the trees. He broke in downstairs. He found her working all alone in her office.

Maureen clutched the bannister. In her mind, the memory of a dream. Kneeling before the dark figure and begging for her life. Reaching out as the blade of the knife came flashing towards her. Screaming her husband's name, knowing that she would never see him again.

The building has been disused ever since then, the people said, the people who still came here sometimes: the cleaners and the caretakers and the police. *It's been disused for years. Because of the stories. The stories told by the people on the trains.*

The trains that come past here every day.

Maureen staggered through the doors into the fourth floor, the unused, deserted floor that was filled with the ghosts of her life, memories of people who were once real, who would still be real if only she could awake from this dream. She ran into her office, to the desk where she had spent so much of her life. The desk where she belonged, where she was safe from the terrible thing in her mind.

A dream, she told herself. *I'm safe, I'm all right. It's just a dream.*

The lights of a train suddenly shone through the darkening night.

He murdered her, the people said. *And sometimes, on darkening nights, when you're sitting on a train that goes right past the building, you can see right into the office where she died. So many people have seen it.*

From the window of the train, you can see...

As the lights blazed against the yellowed glass, Maureen saw the mirror image of the office behind her, and inside that office stood a nightmare shape, a thing with long, bonelike arms and a bloody, skull shaped face filled with grinning teeth.

You can see her phantom standing at the window.

Maureen stared at the gaping, blood drenched eye sockets until the vision was ripped away, the sound of the train charging into the distance, dragging the image it had conjured into the depths of her decaying mind.

For a moment, she felt as if she was waking from a dream.

What was that? she thought. *What just happened?*

She grasped at the memory.

The trains...

Something about the trains.

She turned away from the window. She had to get on with her work. It was quarter past four, and already nearly dark. The nights were drawing in. As she sat down, she was struck by the feeling that there was something just beyond her grasp.

Or perhaps it was just the memory of a dream.

On a Front Porch on a November Afternoon

M. Regan

I'M BAD AT FINDING THINGS.

So bad.

Really, it's kind of ridiculous how bad, and that's a point I want to drive home—sorry, poor word choice—except I'm not sure how. I mean, you probably don't need me to. Or want me to. It's a common enough failing to just accept, isn't it? That I'm basically shit at all forms of hide-and-seek?

I've always been like that, too. Toys, pens, books, sunglasses. Once, I managed to lose my laptop for two weeks because it blended so well with the ottoman. I nearly had a breakdown over that. So yesterday, when I realized my iPhone wasn't in my pocket after leaving

Trader Joe's...*Christ*—it felt like the wind had been punched clean out of me.

I backtracked. Right then. Obviously, I backtracked. My arms were full of groceries, but perishables be damned. Spoiled yogurt and melted ice cream meant nothing in the face of potential identity theft. Or, you know, the expense of buying a new phone.

So. There I was, paper bag dampening in my arms and legs shuffling through scattered leaves, trying to sift through things with my feet. I figured there was a chance my phone had slipped from my pocket during my initial trek home and had gotten buried, but the further I went the slimmer that chance became. I was already almost back to where I'd been when I first noticed it was missing, and I hadn't seen a hint of it.

Wait, please. You'll want to hear this.

A bleeding autumn sunset strobed through the chain-link fence that I was trudging beside, its rays flashing in my periphery. The headache I could feel forming between my eyes was doing nothing for my mood, and knowing that I'd soon be losing daylight didn't help matters, either.

Panic set in. I swore. Colorfully. And of course, the moment I did, I realized there was a *boy* playing in the park on the other side of the fence.

From what I could see, there was no one else around—no siblings or babysitters or even other kids—but after the kind of day I'd had, the last thing I needed was a parent popping out of the woodwork to lay into me over their second grader's delicate ears. Sure, the kid seemed distracted by whatever game he was playing, but that game brought him pretty close to me and the fence, and in my experience little boys hear only what they shouldn't and nothing else.

I bit my tongue, abandoned my groceries, and began digging through the leaves in earnest.

It was six by this point. Twilight was starting to eclipse sundown, which was bad for me, because I really needed that light. The nearest streetlamp was on the other side of the fence, inside the park itself, and only strong enough to make the community bulletin board legible. Had I some weird urge to decipher the sun-bleached and rain-washed poster scraps still tacked to moldering plywood, it might've done me some good, but I didn't, so it didn't.

Anyway. The quarter hour I had before the crimson dusk hemorrhaged into true night kept me focused on my business. The boy kept to his. Who could say what he was doing or why? From what bits of his game I half-noticed, it involved a lot of poking his head into playground tubes and jumping behind dried shrubs. It didn't make sense to me. The games that children play rarely make sense.

There's a lot in life that doesn't make sense. *This* doesn't make sense. None of this makes sense, it *doesn't*, and somehow, I can't help believing it only happened the way it did because I didn't have my phone.

Stuff like this, *unbelievable* stuff, it only ever happens when there's no way to record it, no way for people to prove they aren't crazy, no way to show others it actually happened.

But it *actually happened.*

"You playing, too?"

That was him. That was what he said to me. He'd come up to the fence while I was crawling around and had curled his little fingers between the links, shaking them. The metallic jangle startled me, as did his breezy whisper-scream.

His entire face was shadows. I blinked at him.

"What?"

"You playing, too?" he asked again. The look that I gave him probably wasn't very kind.

"Not now," I told him. Being honest, my attention was already back on the grass, so cold and gray and damp beneath the leaves. "I'm busy."

"Okay! That's okay." The boy—boy-shape—was very reassuring. I still couldn't make out any of his features, but I could hear him smiling. I could also hear when something serious crept into his voice, though I didn't take it particularly seriously.

He said, "If you're not gonna play yet, don't tell me if you see her, okay?"

He added, "If you find her before me, you can't tell. That's cheating. Okay? Don't tell."

"Okay," I agreed, but only to make him go away.

And he did. Go away, that is. Off towards the sandbox, filled with the silhouettes of toy cranes and upturned pails. In the dusk, the dune of it had become a singular black mound.

Leaves hissed around my shins. Sand rasped in the distance. I swear I heard the street lamp's filaments twanging to life, followed by the swelling, unnatural, buzzing glow of its bulb. There was no other sound.

That's why it scares me that I didn't hear anything.

No shouting. No running. There was no reason for me to look up. Just—*silence*. And I didn't notice, *I didn't notice*, until I stood to go back home and there she was.

Right there.

The girl was small, and thin, and grainy. Not like an old picture or a bad movie effect, I mean actually *grainy*. Sand crumbled from her clothes, like ash from used kindling. Sand was matted in her hair, clumpy and discolored. Sand even seemed to have gotten into her joints, stilting the steps she took across the lawn. One, then two, then three, away from the empty play structure, the deserted swings, the vacant sandbox.

I forgot about my phone.

"Hey!" I called, scrambling to the fence. The fields that rolled behind her had been swallowed by the void. Soon, she and I would be lost to it, too. "Hey, you! Where's the other kid? You can't just leave someone you're playing with! He'll worry! If you're going home, go together!"

Grit scratched beneath the girl's soles when she swayed to a stop. That streetlight popped. She wavered in the boundary between light and darkness, a sallow haze hanging around her head, before turning and meeting my eyes with a face scraped clean of detail.

If I hadn't lost my voice to terror, I would have screamed. But I couldn't. And because I didn't, I heard that faceless creature say:

It's his turn to hide. He can go home when he's found.

Behind her, on that rotting bulletin board, dull block text on old scraps of paper whisper-screamed in a breeze: *HAVE YOU SEEN ME?*

Then she kept walking. Or something like walking. And I'm sorry—I'm so sorry—but I ran. I ran faster than I've ever run in my life, and it didn't feel fast enough. I got home and locked the door and didn't sleep a wink, but that wasn't enough to convince me that the girl hadn't been a nightmare. I wanted so badly to believe she was a nightmare.

Sophia Yao wasn't a nightmare.

She's on that bulletin board. The community one. In the park. I saw what was left of her poster this morning, all curdled and blurry, stapled under who-knows-how-many other fliers. *LOST* and *MISSING CHILD* and...

And my phone was there. I don't know how it got there. I don't want to know how it got there. But there it was, behind that damn bulletin board and still at 11% battery. Someone—something—had opened it to my Facebook feed, where the local news station had made a recent post about a child who'd finally come home.

Two years later, her parents said, and Sophia was finally back on their doorstep, broken and decomposing.

I don't know what else to tell you. I understand that this sounds crazy. *I* sound crazy, and I can't do or say or show you anything to prove that I'm not. But I—I thought you should know what I saw. I thought you should know what happened. I thought you should know that I dug to the bottom of that sandbox—frantic, hands flying, like a person possessed—and found nothing hidden there. Just a shallow concrete foundation.

This is going to take me a while. Really, I am so bad at finding things.

I'm sorry I can't tell you where your son is yet.

The End of the World and a Super 88

Michael Ezell

THE RADIO IN MARTIN'S UNIT let out the three quick beeps that always preceded an all-hands emergency call less than five minutes into his meal break. The last few months, he'd begun to hear those beeps in his nightmares.

Beep-beep-beep!

All Southside units, numerous calls of Crusaders charging down Fifth Street at Hanover Mall. Full armor and horses. Multiple civilian casualties.

Martin sighed and threw his chili dog out the window. He didn't even get a bite. What the hell ever happened to a solid Union lunch break? He hit the lights and siren and squealed out of the parking lot of Curly Moe's Hot Dogs.

Best in the City, their slogan read—which really wasn't the claim it once was, given what little was left of the city.

At over a hundred miles per hour, people became blurred fence posts on the sidewalks, and Martin's gut clenched tight enough to make him happy he missed out on the chili dog. There were days when he fleetingly wished a garbage truck would pull out in front of him and end it right there. Ugly way to go, but he was about to see uglier, of that he was sure.

Oh shit.

He hit the brakes at Fifth and Hanover hard enough to make them burn.

"Dear Lord," he said, as much a prayer as an exclamation.

Civilians ran screaming everywhere; an overturned Corvette, a UPS truck, and a minivan burned in the intersection where they'd crashed together. The fire generated a furious tower of oily black smoke, marring the sky like black ink spilled on flawless blue paper. Several armored horses were down, and two-dozen others skittered about in the growing pools of blood on the asphalt. A gruesome swath of dead civilians radiated outward from the smoking line on Fifth Street where the Rip had spit out the Crusaders.

Fifty knights on horseback, even with ancient weaponry, were a horrifying force.

Corpses of massacred shoppers littered the street right up until the point where the first police car arrived. The line of the battle turned back from there, leaving dead horses and maimed Crusaders with bullet holes punched in their shining armor.

Martin snatched his assault rifle out of the rack and took cover behind his vehicle. Across the street, a rookie named Jenkins banged away with his handgun, panicky shots as likely to whack a civilian as a Crusader. The kid ran his pistol dry and his sweaty fingers dropped his new magazine during the reload. A knight on his side of the street who had narrowly escaped being gunned down by the rookie wheeled his battle horse onto the sidewalk. They may not have had Glocks in 1200 AD, but the wily old warrior knew a man having troubles with his weapon when he saw one. He spurred his mount and charged Jenkins.

Martin popped off two quick shots, but only shattered the back windows of a bus stalled in the street. As the thundering hooves got closer and closer to Jenkins, Martin clicked the selector to Full Auto and squeezed off a burst—and blew out the front window of a jewelry store, adding the earsplitting *ree-ree-ree* of an alarm to the insanity.

Jenkins made a fatal mistake. He stopped reloading and looked up when he heard galloping hooves. If he'd kept reloading, he could've at least gotten off a shot or two.

The knight's broadsword whistled around in a deadly arc and cleaved Jenkins' head from his left jaw to his right ear. The Crusader then yanked his horse around and charged Martin.

Martin screamed in rage and fear. He fired everything he had left in one long, ripping burst. Knight and horse tumbled into the street like a wave of crashing armor, weapons, and flesh, cresting and dying at his front bumper. He slapped in another magazine and slowly stepped out from behind his car, heart hammering so hard he felt like his eyes would pop out of his head.

Gun up, he moved to check on the Crusader. Nothing but a bloody mess below the metal nose protector of his helmet. One less Crusader on Fifth Street tonight.

The ripping growl of an electric Gatling gun announced the arrival of SWAT.

From here, the battle would be short. SWAT carried grenade launchers and two of the big Gatlings. No matter how dedicated to the Pope these Crusaders were, those modern-day heathens were mowin' 'em down.

Watching the defiant last stand of the surviving Crusaders, Martin wondered if it would get easier some day, if he'd be able to take the slaughter with that passive look on his face, like Norm Sabine. An old-school *veterano*, Norm had seen it all. Nothing could make him spit out the chew in his lip, or break the cowboy-on-the-range expression he always wore.

Martin retrieved the Crusader's jeweled broadsword and wiped the blood on the dead knight's tunic. He thought he saw the top of Jenkins's head out of the corner of his eye, but he told himself he didn't.

He tossed the sword with its bejeweled handle into his trunk, securing the glimmering prize from hungry eyes. The consequences of keeping objects that appeared through a Rip were brutal—and so was the punishment for keeping anything. He fought those consequences all the time. If so much as one thing from a specific time or different plane of existence stayed here, it seemed to be a magnet for more things or people from that time or dimension. A nameless Homeland Security agent had delivered the only official briefing Martin ever heard on the Rips, maybe six months after the things started appearing. The government wasn't sure whether this was some scientific accident, terrorism, or black magic, but DHS was damn sure about one thing: keep nothing that came out of a Rip. Upon pain of death.

The bodies of the Crusaders, their horses, armor, weapons, every last scrap had to be destroyed in the furnaces at the dump. If some crackhead got his hands on this jeweled sword and scattered the stones around town, they'd be fighting Crusaders for months.

The shooting finally died down and Martin drove his unit into position to help cordon off the block. Someone was already going around taking orders for coffee. It would be a long night of watching City Maintenance scrape Crusaders and horse guts off the street.

Martin put his visor down against the setting sun and pretended not to see Corporal Halverson quietly weeping behind the wheel of his patrol car. That's how it went. When you saw another cop break down, you ignored it.

It was the decent thing to do.

The streetlights seemed unnaturally bright tonight. He could clearly see squadrons of biting flies circling the mounds of garbage along the curb. Was there any surer sign of the modern world's demise than uncollected garbage?

Martin hadn't walked a foot beat since he was a rookie, and he felt good in the cool night air. All the businesses were shut tight and the brownstones only had one or two lights on at this hour. The lack of the city's usual light pollution let him view the stars glittering overhead like shattered diamonds. The quiet solitude of the night shift could be a glorious thing.

When he hit the corner of Almond and Delaware, he spotted old Norm Sabine leaning against the fender of his police car and eating something. Looked like nachos with salsa.

Norm scooped with a chip, popped it into his mouth, and winked at Martin.

"Hey, Norm, didn't the wife put you on a heart-healthy diet? You're not supposed to be eating nachos," Martin said.

Norm gave Martin his old cowboy-on-the-range look and put another chip in his mouth. Something seemed odd about the chip, about what was on it. With gut-wrenching suddenness, Martin realized Norm wasn't eating salsa and cheese out of a paper bowl. He was using corn chips to eat brains out of the off-kilter slice of Jenkins' skull.

Martin turned to puke—

—And woke up with rising gorge in his throat.

He scrambled out of bed and into the bathroom before he let go. Almost made it to the toilet. The splattering sound on the tile and the warm splash on his feet made him throw up more. At least this time, he got it in the sink.

Stumbling to the kitchen, he turned the cold tap on full and sluiced fresh water through his mouth to get rid of the acid bile taste. He couldn't bring himself to face the cleanup in the bathroom, so he wiped the splashes of vomit off his feet with a dishtowel and downed half a glass of milk to prepare his stomach for what was coming.

One sure way to a dreamless sleep was half a bottle of Johnny Walker Red and something from the smorgasbord of confiscated prescription drugs under his kitchen sink. He went to the window and stared at the street four stories down. Nothing moved except an armored truck from Metro SWAT. They'd be on high alert for at least two more days. Department policy mandated three days of high alert after a Rip event.

Jenkins flashed into his mind again. Young and smiling, the first time Martin saw him in the briefing room. Fresh out of the academy, still thinking he'd do some good.

Martin had to take a few whooping deep breaths to keep from bursting into tears. Damn kid had eight months on the job. He'd signed up after all the shit started, not like Martin, Norm Sabine, and every other veteran of more than five years. The kid had balls. Big brass ones.

How much longer could they do this? No one could find an answer, not all the Pope's people or all the President's men—not even that twelve year-old Chinese kid who could beat a computer in math. So they kept slaughtering whatever came out of those Rips. Fighting to the end, which seemed likely to come soon. As Jenkins found out, sometimes the slaughter went both ways.

Martin washed down a Percocet with a double shot of JW Red. Dr. Soorani, the department shrink, told him he shouldn't feel guilt about doing his job. Only violent people or creatures came out of those Rips. Government scientists had confirmed it as fact.

He poured a hefty dollop of brown fire into his glass and strolled into his tiny living room. He went through a ritual he'd developed over many sleepless nights. Circling the room counter-clockwise, he examined all the photos on the walls one by one. Him and his parents, in better times.

Three-year-old Martin standing on the hood of his dad's pride and joy, a red and white 1959 Oldsmobile Super 88 Holiday.

A candid snap of his mom and dad decorating the Christmas tree.

His parents at a Halloween party. Dad in a terrible Frankenstein's monster outfit, the green makeup stopping about halfway down his neck, and Mom in a Gryffindor robe with a drawn-on lighting bolt scar on her forehead.

A picture of Martin and his parents at his Police Academy graduation...

For the first time, he broke from his ritual. He took the Academy picture off its hook and held it close to his eyes, as if it could tell him the secret to understanding all this. Then he opened the window and tossed it out, watching it spin until it smashed on the street below.

He went to the closet and grabbed his old Browning Auto 5 shotgun. Three thousand rounds of twelve-gauge ammo, including a thousand rifled slugs, were the only remnants of his Doomsday armory. He traded the rest of the shit to an evidence technician for two cases of JW Red, a bag of questionable Quaaludes, and a signed Les Paul guitar. Hell, he didn't even play. He'd given up hoping for long-term survival back when the government told the Chief there would be no more troops to help them fight. Every city became a lone outpost, expected to fend for itself. Martin mainly used the boxes of shells for doorstops and such now.

Between sips of whiskey, he broke down the shotgun on the coffee table, cleaned it, and put it back together. Once he finished, he started over. It kept his mind occupied until the pills and booze could bushwhack him.

His head nodded forward as he ran a cloth over the old shotgun's barrel. He thought of his parent's last moments. Had they gotten the weird wavering-consciousness feeling when the drugs took hold, too? Of course, Martin would wake up in the morning, a little hung over, but still here. They hadn't been willing to deal with waking up again.

Had they hit upon the best solution, in the end? Should he dive into a deep sleep and never come up for air, instead of slogging through blood and guts, living with sheer terror every day until something un-killable came through a Rip or a Crusader turned his head into a dip bowl? He swirled the last of the whiskey in his glass and used it to wash down another Percocet, not really caring whether he woke up tomorrow.

Like someone stuffed ground glass into a sandwich bag.

That's how his brain felt. Martin cursed himself for both the whiskey, and the extra Percocet. He drove along in the slow lane, sunglasses jammed right up against his eyes to ward off the mid-morning sun. His mouth was full of cotton, but the wheel of his old man's '59 Olds Super 88 Holiday felt cool and smooth in his hands.

His grandpa bought it new off the showroom floor, and through a weekend tradition of washing, waxing, and buffing, kept it looking brand-new for decades, passing it on to Martin's dad, who kept up the same fanatical devotion to the bright red 88. He probably would have wept to see the door dings and the faded paint now.

The red and white monstrosity was bad enough to drive in light traffic. Today, it seemed like everyone had taken the Rip as a sign to get out and get some pre-apocalypse shopping done. Martin put up with the assholes in traffic, because he felt like if he screamed at someone, he'd throw up. So he sat. Inched forward. And sat. The reward for his nauseated patience was a patio table outside El Rey's, a cold beer, and some side jalapenos for his steaming bowl of menudo. He always liked to burn the badness out of himself after a night like last night. It never really worked, but at least it got rid of the hangover.

As he ate, he watched cars go by. Skittish drivers hunched over steering wheels, hyper-vigilant, eyes looking everywhere. Not for a guy running a stop sign, but for a Nazi tank, or alien submarine, or some other crazy thing that would suddenly turn your car and your nice normal life into a flaming heap of shit.

But we hold our heads up and keep going, Martin thought. *Because that's what we do, right? If we don't then…somebody wins and it isn't us, so we damn well don't give up.* Well, some did. Like his parents, lying with their fingers intertwined in one last cold embrace.

The thought made Martin shiver, an edgy panic attack lurking in the back of his mind. He turned his gaze up to the rainbow table umbrella shading him. He was sure if he looked down at the bowl of menudo, he would—

It was going to happen anyway.

He ran around the little taco shack and threw up behind the dumpster. The smell there made his stomach continue to roll, so he staggered away, gasping for fresh air. A young mother with a kid in a stroller looked at him like he was some filthy junkie. She had a bag of groceries stuffed in the basket under the stroller. She'd made her banzai run for groceries and was headed back for cover. Martin knew the feeling. Only he never got to head back for cover.

He went to his car and snagged a bottle of water off the front seat. As he swished the nasty taste out of his mouth, he watched the young mother make her way to the crosswalk. She looked left, right, then did a double take right.

Letting out a screech of sheer terror, she pushed her stroller right out into traffic. Cars skidded everywhere, but she paid them no mind. She pushed the stroller for all she was worth, wheels scuffing and sliding as she ran, screaming all the way.

There was a time when Martin would have wondered what made her scream.

He already had the 88's trunk open. More from habit than necessity, he checked the load in the Browning shotgun. The magazine tube was full of double-ought buckshot; each shell contained nine .33 caliber lead balls. He had five rifled slugs in a butt-stock bandoleer, and he grabbed a belt with extra buckshot held in elastic loops.

The warning sirens already started by the time Martin heard a crackling, electrical *boom* that sounded like a transformer letting go. A Rip had opened somewhere close. Usually, there would be at least a month or two between Rips. Aftershock Rips were rare, but they did happen. *Figures it would have to be on a hangover day.* The odds were always against him there.

Without thinking, Martin gunned the old '88 toward the sound. Stupid. He should be driving the other way. Off duty, no vest, no radio, no assault rifle, and no common sense. Dr. Soorani encouraged them to report fellow officers if they started doing things to purposely put themselves in harm's way. Hell, that described showing up to work these days.

Martin kept his windows down like a good cop, listening for signs of where the bad stuff was happening. He followed the sounds of sirens down the concrete canyons leading into the business district. From there, the screams told him where to go. He knew it was bad when he saw the eternal hard-ass Norm Sabine on his knees in the middle of the street, screeching like a girl in a horror movie. Martin had read enough Tolkien to give a name to the thing that had torn off Norm's left arm.

Orc.

Big mean fuckers with green hide and thick teeth. Their bows were taller than a man; their arrows, three feet long and thick as a broomstick. They pinned cops to their units, split heads and charged on to bury themselves in innocent civilians too slow to get into the bus stop bunkers.

Martin stepped out through his driver's door and found himself entranced in the midst of all the horror. Not by the orcs, but by the warriors fighting the orcs. Slender and tall, armored in gold and silver, they rode magnificent white horses with breathtaking agility. After years of seeing what the Rips spit out, he had no doubt they were elves. Badass elves, too. They used recurve bows to shoot silver-tipped arrows at the orcs. Deadly, graceful, every arrow bringing down an enemy. They probably would have won the fight, if two armored trucks full of SWAT cops who didn't give a damn which side won hadn't showed up.

Roaring electric Gatlings and automatic grenade launchers laid waste to orcs and Elven riders alike. The battle broke up as survivors scattered, trying to make sense of this strange new world and the new enemies slaughtering them. A rider broke away and galloped up the sidewalk straight toward Martin.

He threw the shotgun to his shoulder and put the front sight on the rider's chest. Easy squeeze on the trigger...

An orc leaped out of an alley and landed astride the horse's neck. The horse twisted and bucked, threatening to throw off both its rider and the orc. The rider slashed at the orc with a long dagger as the horse faltered and staggered into the alley out of Martin's sight.

The fight down the street raged on as something new came out of the Rip. A battalion of orcs with catapults that launched vessels filled with black fire. One of the SWAT trucks went supernova when the black fire licked inside and hit the spare high-explosive ammo. Cops in heavy tactical armor were scattered like bleeding candlepins.

The sound of clanging blades drew Martin toward the alleyway. He nearly got crushed when the Elven warrior's horse rocketed out of the opening without its rider. Now he could see the rider and orc engaged in desperate combat. He decided to hang back and let them damage each other as much as possible. He'd take care of the winner.

Tall, well over six feet but not exactly broad-shouldered, the elf wielded a slender blade that *sang* when it whipped through the air. The orc, on the other hand, was over seven feet tall, all muscle, and brandished a broadsword as big a Cadillac's bumper.

Brawn proved to be the decisive edge. The elf was losing the battle, slowly but surely. A glancing blow knocked the elf's helmet off and slammed her onto her back—

Her.

Golden hair matted with sweat, high spots of red coloring the fairest cheeks Martin had ever seen. With a victory roar, the orc raised his sword for the coup de grace.

Martin shot him in the back. A lot. Five rounds of double-ought buckshot in two seconds, like rolling thunderclaps in the alley.

And did it ever piss off the orc.

He roared at Martin and set his feet to charge. Black spittle flew from his lips and bluish blood from the gunshot wounds spattered on the alley floor. Martin didn't see much of it. Having learned from the Jenkins moment, he had his head down and was busy shoving all five rifled slugs into the shottie's magazine.

The orc charged him with a battle cry loud enough to rattle Martin's teeth and nearly make him wet his pants. The beast pulled up short with a howl of pain as the Elven warrior slashed her blade across the orc's hamstrings. Instead of going down, he spun and smashed the brave elf across the head with his sword's massive pommel.

This bought Martin all the time he needed.

When the orc raised his sword to behead the beautiful elf, Martin shot him through the armpit with a rifled twelve-gauge slug. Mystical creature or not, nobody shrugs that off.

The orc slumped against the alley wall and actually looked at Martin in surprise.

"Yeah, I know the feeling," Martin said. Rapid-fire, he put all four remaining slugs through the orc's face. The stinking beast sagged to the alley floor, its black brains splashed all over the wall.

Reloading the smoking shotgun from his belt of buckshot rounds, Martin approached the unconscious elf. He knew what he had to do. There were rules, after all. He stopped cold when he got a good look at her face. Fine blue veins ran across her temples, her skin so fair he imagined he could see the blood pumping through. He knelt and looked at the bloody wound in her blond hair. He was shocked to find the bleeding had already stopped. Apparently, elves were made of stern stuff.

Knowing he shouldn't but unable to stop himself, he brushed his fingertips across her cheek, hesitantly touching a flawless pointed ear. Still out cold, she sighed. The sound was so musical it made his skin tingle.

Automatic weapons fire from down the block reminded him of where he was and what had to happen from here. He had never encountered someone who survived long enough to be taken into custody, but he knew what would happen. He'd heard the rumors. Special warehouses run by the Feds for "living subjects" recovered from Rip events. People from the Rips went in, and none of them ever came out.

Technically, Martin was supposed to shoot her right here and now. Otherwise, the entire city was in danger of orc invasions and who knew what else. He looked at her pale face, the achingly perfect bow of her lips, and his heart told him what would happen long before he formed the actual thought.

He sprinted back to get his car, and threw the shotgun in the back seat. Things were settling down now and he saw numerous on-duty cops moving to cordon off the area for the cleanup sweep. Cranking up the '88, he tried to drive casually. The last thing he needed was to chirp the tires and make uniforms look his way. He halfway hoped she'd be gone when he got back so he wouldn't be able to do this crazy shit.

He drove past the alley then backed in. When he jumped out, he heard a black and white coming up the street, its PA system blaring, "This area is off-limits until further notice."

Although she was tall, she seemed to weigh nothing, as if her body was some special magical thing he shouldn't even be touching. He laid her across his back seat and threw his jacket over her. *Yeah, great idea.* Muscular legs clad in golden shin guards still stuck out. Martin shrugged and slid behind the wheel.

He pulled out of the alley a little too fast and nearly got t-boned by a police unit. The driver jumped out and slammed his door. "You dumb son of a bitch!"

"Hey, Eddie, it's me," Martin yelled.

Eddie Polson had joined the force a year after Martin, and still wore the same flattop haircut he had the day he'd graduated the Academy. "Marty Hernandez, is that you? What are you doin', man?" Eddie walked toward the Olds and Martin's heart trip-hammered. He rolled forward a bit to give the impression he was in a hurry.

"Hey, man, I got caught up in the shit while I was off duty and this big ugly bastard with green skin and bad breath jumped outta nowhere." Martin jerked a thumb back toward the alley. "I shot the shit out of him with my shotgun and finally put him down. But I'm outta ammo, so I'm outta here."

Eddie literally shivered. "I hear you. Those things made me piss my pants. And holy shit, Marty! Norm Sabine...They pulled him apart."

Martin pretended he didn't see the tears rolling down Eddie's face. "Yeah, yeah, I saw. Helluva thing, Ed, helluva thing."

"Yeah."

They both waited the appropriate amount of time to respect Norm's memory.

"Well, I'm headin' back to my place for more ammo. You mind makin' sure the cleanup crew tags the one in the alley for me?" Martin said.

"Sure, sure, no worries. Later, man," Eddie said.

Martin was already on the gas, heading home, the smell of her filling the car like some holy flower on a mountaintop in a pristine, unspoiled country.

His mind was anywhere but where it should have been. It should have been on the wavering, sparkling air two hundred yards from the front sight of his M-60 machinegun.

Sergeant Cisneros from SWAT knelt behind a hastily abandoned Prius in the intersection to Martin's left. In his heavy body armor, the short, muscular veteran looked like a Latino fireplug someone had armed with an antique Browning automatic rifle. They were down to National Guard surplus weapons against whatever magical onslaught the orcs chose to bring this time. And it would be orcs again. And again. Until the detectives from Cleanse and Purge found the object someone kept from the first incursion. Rumor was an Elven king fell during the battle and his crown was pure gold studded with magic stones, something no one could resist.

Martin glanced left and right, his guilty conscience making him wonder if his compatriots were going over the event in their minds, trying to figure out where the perpetrator had access. Of course they weren't even remotely thinking about it. Their sweaty faces were filled with dread, their eyes locked dead ahead.

There were eighty officers in all, gathered around a fairly small Pre-Rip Event in the business district. Sometimes they got lucky and saw a Rip coming because of the sparkly air. Civilians knew to report these things at all costs. Four blocks in every direction had been evacuated and a hasty ambush was thrown together in a half-circle south of the wavering air.

The empty streets were silent and eighty nervous fingers hovered over triggers. Grim faces peered from under riot helmets and military surplus Kevlar brain buckets.

It was likely a good thing none of them saw Martin's goofy grin. At the very least, they'd have him yanked off the streets for evaluation. On a more personal level, happy cops weren't very popular in a world where people's buddies were getting mowed down or torn apart or struck by magic fucking lighting every other day.

But he didn't care. He'd left behind the plane of existence where Martin cared about the desires of other humans the first time he held her in his arms, the first time he wandered lost in the ethereal flower smell of her flawless skin. They hadn't been able to understand each other at first. Martin got as far as her name. *Luzon*. At least, that was close. She had smiled when he repeated it, so there you go. He spent three hours digging through a pile of old software in an abandoned Best Buy and came up with a Rosetta Stone program for English. He left it running on his laptop when he went to work and hoped for the best.

Within two shifts, she was having halting conversations with him. Martin felt like a talented circus monkey next to her. He couldn't even remember the Elvish words for "cup" or "knife." They seemed slippery somehow, like he was never meant to know them, and he couldn't get them to stick in his mind. But seeing her every day kept her name in his mind. That was all he cared about.

He knew none of these guys would ever understand him allowing her to live, much less sheltering her. He also knew he had to do something about it. Soon. Being in her presence was like jolting awake after a long, dark nightmare, and he never wanted to go back. Maybe it was madness, this plan of his, but his old life had already been spiraling to an end. Why not try something different, even if it was something people would say was totally mental?

Could you really call his idea a plan, though? "Suicidal notion" might be better.

With a crackling boom, the Rip opened, spiking his system with so much adrenaline, spots danced in his vision. Time to clock in. He squeezed his trigger and the M-60 hammered staccato death into the ranks of charging orcs.

As incursions go, it wasn't too horrible. No more than a hundred orcs. The early going was dicey, because the front rank of orcs rode armored nightmare beasts, overgrown elephants with T-Rex heads. This buckled the police lines for a moment, because ten rookies freaked out and ran, but Cisneros and Martin were not only veteran cops, they were veterans of Rip incursions. They both had the same idea. They turned their heavy guns on the legs of the armored beasts, teaching the orcs a free lesson about armor piercing ammunition.

Stupid orcs.

Heading back home, the '88 rolled along the dark streets with hardly anyone to challenge it. Since the main Rip when Martin found Luzon, they'd had ever-increasing orc incursions from aftershock Rips. Everyone still alive knew the reason for such things, and there were roving bands of vigilantes smashing pawnshops, tracking down drug addicts and beating false confessions out of them. This generated fear of being caught out alone by one of the mobs, so most civilians stayed off the streets after dark.

Martin opened up the Oldsmobile's throaty 394 and let it run. The old girl might be getting on in years, but she still growled like a hot rod when she wanted to, and he was more than happy to get home twice as fast tonight.

A short blip of a siren and spinning lights behind him yanked him back to reality. He pulled over nice and easy. Within seconds, a flashlight shined in his eyes and Martin saw the muzzle of a pistol. "Easy, easy, I'm off duty!"

"What the hell, Marty? The way you were haulin' ass, I thought someone stole your car and was out joyriding in it." The flashlight went out and Eddie Polson blinked at Martin in the sudden darkness.

"Thanks for the concern, Ed. I think," Martin said.

Eddie looked uncomfortable, but said it anyway. "Didn't see you at Norm's funeral."

"Yeah, I just couldn't take another one, man. Folded flags and fuckin' bagpipes playing 'Amazing Grace.' Can't do it anymore."

"I hear ya, I hear ya. Hey, how you guys doin' on Day Watch? We got these freakin' orc things poppin' up left and right."

Now Martin looked uncomfortable. "Uh, had a nasty one today. But they let us start carrying heavy machineguns in our trunks, so that helped."

"No more elves, though, huh? I mean, you seen any since that first time?" Eddie said.

"What? Why? I mean, no." Martin knew he was stammering, but the question caught him by surprise. He'd heard guys talking about the disappearance of elves from the latest incursions, but no one had ever asked him directly.

Eddie gave him a dead-eyed stare, staying silent for so long, Martin started to squirm, until he finally realized Eddie was staring *through* him. Finally, Eddie blinked and roused himself, like a man remembering the shreds of a foggy dream. He sounded bone-tired. "Night before last, we lost three rookies. Dumb-asses froze up, and this big damn orc with at least fifty bullets in him tore 'em apart. Bit one guy's face off."

Eddie's voice shrank up and cracked at the end. He held up a hand and walked toward the back bumper. When Martin heard him sobbing, he kept his gaze on the windshield and waited. It was the decent thing to do. Shortly, Eddie came back. His pale cheeks made two days of beard stubble stand out. Martin hadn't really noticed the eye-bags and deep lines before. Eddie looked so worn out, he could almost see through him.

"You look happy, Martin," Eddie said, his voice gravelly and low.

"Uh...what?"

"Why is that? Why the fuck are you so happy lately? Lots of guys have noticed."

Martin glared back at Eddie. He was a long damn way from happy yet, and he could trade empty stares with anyone out here. Calmly, he said, "Hey, Eddie, it seems quiet tonight. Why don't you cruise back to the station and tell the L-T you're sick. Go home, drink a beer, and get some righteous sleep, man."

The hard edges broke and Eddie's face fell into a lined mask of exhaustion. "Martin, I tell you the truth. I don't believe I'll ever get any righteous sleep again. Not ever." He patted the roof of the '88 by way of goodbye, and wandered back to his patrol car.

Martin put his Super '88 in gear and pointed it toward his baby.

Back at his apartment, she had their gear squared away and ready to roll. Of course, she did. She was a flawless warrior and the owner of his heart. The M-60 from his police unit was in a black canvas bag close to the door. The guys in the department armory had long ago stopped caring who turned in their guns at End of Watch. Everyone had weapons and food stockpiled. It was what humans did at the end of the world.

The other guns were in their rigs and ready to strap on. He'd taught her how to handle the guns, and she taught him how to handle her singing sword. Or at least how to swing it without hacking off his own limbs.

He peeked into the bedroom and saw her staring into the duffle bag containing her golden armor. She wore his Chicago Bears sweatshirt and some loose women's jeans he found at a thrift shop. And she looked more spectacular than any model Martin ever laid eyes on.

She ran her fingers over the strange lettering on the armor and her eyes were far away. She seemed so out of place in this ramshackle little bachelor's pad with the peeling linoleum and cobwebs in the corners. Tall, gangly, but possessing an unearthly strength that sometimes scared him. Her hair wasn't blond, it was a vision of some fairy tale straw spun into gold. When she whispered his name, the music in her voice drove him mad.

Luzon turned and pinned him with her silver eyes. "How was your day?"

He smiled at her. "You don't have to say that every time I go out and come back. You can just say 'Hi' if you want."

She grinned and gave him a kiss on the forehead. "Hi."

"Ready to head out on patrol, soldier?" Martin said.

"Aye, aye, sir," she said.

"That's a sailor."

"Well, the machine you drive is not unlike a boat," Luzon said.

"Good point. Let's hit the road, sailor."

Ever since she told him the Rips were happening on her side too, he had been turning this idea over and over in his mind, worried he was insane and he'd only get them killed. The deciding factor was that she was desperate to go home, and he was desperate to never be without her. From there, the choices were pretty limited.

Their normal routine was to pack up every night and cruise what was left of the open highways around town, her wearing a beanie to hide her ears, like Mr. Spock gone time traveling. They were hoping to spot a Pre-Rip Event and time the opening moment exactly right. Martin's brilliant plan was to gun the old '88 for all she was worth and drive right into the Rip. They weren't killing everything that came through in her world. They were trying to form some sort of coalition to figure out what was happening and how they could fix it. If they could fix it.

Driving around in downtown areas was dicey. Martin himself was part of a team made up of veteran Day Watch officers who routinely shook down every gangster, every snitch, every crackhead, looking for an imaginary object Martin knew didn't exist.

Knowing the truth, he felt terrible guilt over the people who lost their lives when the Rips continued to spit out orcs and their horrible devices of war, but what was he supposed to do, turn Luzon over to be shot and cremated?

Did it really matter if the Rips spit out orcs, dragons, or Nazis? Dead was dead.

Luzon put her arms around him and pulled him close. "You do not required to do this."

"Do not *have to* do this. And yes, I do. Lookit, you're the first thing in years that has made me smile. There's no end to this shit. Someday something's gonna come through a Rip that's gonna eat this whole damn world." He ran his fingers through the cool silk of her hair. "If I'm gonna go out, I'd rather do it at the wheel of a 1959 Olds Super '88, with my arm around a gorgeous blond I'm crazy about."

"But we hope to not go out. Correct?" Luzon said.

Martin laughed out loud and it made him feel so fucking good, he almost wept. "Yeah, the plan is to not go out at all."

It was almost dawn when Luzon spotted the sparkly lines in the sky. A Rip was forming, no more than ten blocks away. Martin swooped the old red and white battleship across three lanes and roared down the off-ramp. Luzon leaned forward in her seat, as if she could already see the beautiful forests and cities of stone and wood she told him about.

"Lock and load," he said.

She smiled and snapped a magazine into his rifle. She chambered a round and pointed the muzzle at the floorboard. Martin knew they'd probably have a hell of a fight to get near the Rip. Special Response Teams roamed the streets now, everyone on edge since the Rips became more and more frequent. He hoped and prayed they'd only have to fight orcs to get through. He didn't want to have to make the other decision—

Another short blip of a siren staggered his heartbeat and the spinning lights made him sick to his stomach. Luzon's eyes glowed silver in the spotlight when she looked back, and he damn near stomped on the gas and went for it, but they needed to be closer to the Rip before he tried it. If they ran now, the cop behind them would simply get on the radio and those response teams would be waiting for them with a lot more than two machineguns.

"Put my jacket over the rifle and be still," Martin said.

No sooner had Luzon dropped the jacket into place than Martin was staring into a bright light. The light went out and he wished he were still looking at brilliant white nothing rather than the dead eyes behind the sights of Eddie's pistol.

"Who is she, Marty? And don't bullshit me." Eddie leaned down and stared at Luzon's ethereal beauty. "She ain't from here."

By *here*, Martin knew he didn't even mean this universe, much less this town.

"Damn, Eddie. I thought you were supposed to get some sleep, man."

"It's you, isn't it? I remembered you coming out of the alley, but I thought maybe you kept some of that gold or silver. I figured you were happy because you were gonna try to buy your way to Tahiti or someplace where this isn't happening."

"There's nowhere this isn't happening, man. It's happening where she's from, too," Martin said.

Eddie blinked at Luzon as if he just recognized she was a real person. "Oh... Uh, good evening, ma'am."

Luzon knocked him dizzy with her smile. "How was your day?"

Eddie shot Martin a look. *Is she for real?*

"Look, this is happening everywhere," Martin said. "But she says there are survivors on her side. They don't automatically kill everyone who comes through. They've banded together over there. And they have other ways of fighting where she's from, very powerful ways."

"What, like wizards and shit?" Eddie snorted.

"Seriously, Eddie?" Martin said.

"Yeah...Guess you got a point."

"Anyway, we're goin' through that Rip, Eddie. You wanna go?" Martin said. He meant it. He'd take as many people as he could pack in the '88's lifeboat of a backseat. Anywhere was better than this city, this time and place.

Eddie actually stepped back from the car. "What? *Into* one of those things? No thanks, man." He still had his gun out, but it wasn't really pointed at anyone now.

Martin put the '88 in gear. "Hey, Eddie, go home and get some sleep, man. Some righteous sleep."

Eddie gave him a hollow stare. He brought the gun up again. Martin and Luzon joined hands and waited. After a few deep breaths, Eddie seemed to sag around his bones. "Yeah, man, maybe I will." He lowered his gun and shuffled back toward his car. Martin let off the brake and rolled away. Looking at Eddie in the rearview mirror, he saw himself back there. A broken, shuffling, zombie of the man he used to be.

And when he turned the corner and saw those charging orcs and the line of guns waiting for them, Martin held his baby tight and gunned that old Super '88 for all she was worth.

Winning in Real Estate
Lara Frater

"WHAT DO YOU MEAN the bulldozers are tangled up?" Sanford "Sandy" Grimes yelled into his cellphone. "Well, untangle them!" He threw the phone down hard against his expensive oak desk, shaking the desk so hard his coffee sloshed and drops spilled. Someone would clean it later, but right now he didn't care.

He sat in his leather chair, then stood and paced his large office on Park Avenue. Yet another stupid problem at his 105th Street work site, the sixth since work started.

He'd gotten the former low-income housing dirt cheap when everything above 96th Street was still considered Harlem, a place where white people feared even driving through.

Now that parts of Harlem were gentrified, filled with chained stores and even a Whole Foods, it attracted rich yuppies and hipsters. He planned to tear it down and put up luxury condos. He expected to make a sweet profit. When his company offered the tenants a buy out, they all accepted at the lowest price without complaint. That surprised him because in previous buildings, he always found some tenants refusing to move: old people set in their ways, people with kids who wanted to stay in the school district, yuppie radicals who thought Sandy oppressed the masses. Sandy didn't give a rat shit about the masses; he wanted to make money. Those who didn't accept a reasonable buy out, Sandy's lawyers always made sure they were screwed at the end.

Sandy sat again and took a long gulp of black coffee and ignored the drops on his desk. His stomach burned. He resisted the urge to throw the cup across the room. He had to be rational about this, but these accidents had been crazy, especially the one the watchmen had just told him about. How could bulldozers get tangled up? They were fucking trucks, for fuck's sake.

He expected the foreman of the building to arrive at any minute. Sandy never met with the help, usually letting intermediates do the work, but he needed to know what the hell was going on.

Tearing the place down hadn't been a problem. When they started building, the accidents began. Cranes malfunctioned, beams fell to the ground, building materials vanished and workers quit for no reason. Sandy never used union laborers, but he always made sure they did a fast job without incidents. Then when the job neared completion, a cable snapped and sent a worker to his death and injured another four. Even though the workers were probably illegals, they all seemed to have beautiful little daughters who cried for their daddies and lawyers.

The press, the police, and the unions were all over him. The union's large inflatable rat became a permanent fixture in front of the worksite, as was a New York Times reporter who seemed to be going for a Pulitzer on the woes of Sandy Grimes. The city issued a stop-work order while the planning commission, the department of buildings, and the police conducted an investigation that Sandy couldn't bribe to go away. His friends started suggesting he sell, he'd still make a big profit and get a tax write off for his losses, but he wasn't giving up without a fight. He realized someone had to be out to get him; a former tenant or some Occupy Crap group.

His intercom rang. The foreman had arrived. Sandy hit the button to open the automatic doors.

Hector Gomez was a small, Hispanic man with a mustache that looked almost invisible on his brown skin. His age, mid-forties, made him a few years older than Sandy. A legalized citizen formerly from Mexico, he had been in the business for a long time and was reliable in getting projects finished by their due date.

Sandy didn't offer him coffee, a chair, or even shake his hand; instead, they stood next to Sandy's desk.

"Hello, Hector." Sandy tried to sound menacing, but Hector didn't seem fazed.

"Hello, Mr. Grimes."

"Can you please tell me what the fuck is going on at 105th Street?"

The swearing had no effect on Hector's demeanor.

"Well?" Sandy asked when Hector didn't respond fast enough.

Hector sighed deeply. "El Diablo."

"Something wrong with the site or someone's sabotaging it?"

"Both."

"Where is this person from? The unions? Some stupid radical? Have they been threatening the workers?"

"The site is hell."

Sandy paused. Hector sounded serious, like he believed the devil caused the problems. While Sandy thought Hector was beneath him in every way, he wasn't a known crazy.

"What are you saying?"

"We work safely, Mr. Grimes. It is the ghosts that cause the problems."

"Ghosts? Are you out of your fucking mind?" Sandy thought Hector had finally gone off his rocker, but he found this too amusing not to run with it.

"Do you know what happened there in the past?" Hector asked. He looked scared but Sandy didn't think it was of him.

"Poor people living in shitty apartments?"

"It was a hospital for the poor. We have disturbed their rest."

Sandy laughed in his face. He, at least, respected Hector for staying calm. "So why the fuck now? Why not when the tenants were living there?"

Hector didn't respond. If what he said had an element of truth, it explained the accidents and why the tenants left without a problem, but Sandy believed in fact not fiction and ghosts did not exist.

"You know what I think, Hector?"

"What, sir?"

"Maybe there's been a bit of drinking on the job?"

"No, sir, I swear. None of my crew ever drinks on the clock. Never. I've done jobs for you several times, sir. I've always done my work. This has never happened before. If you go to the building, you will see."

"I'm sure. Now get out of here. No more drinking on the job or I'll get another crew. Got it?" He might have to replace Hector's company but that would be costly. Maybe if he hired a priest to bless the site, that might make the workers less superstitious. He knew a few padres who owed him favors.

However, Sandy was suspicious now. It couldn't be ghosts. Someone had to be scaring the workers and sabotaging the place. Sandy planned to find out who. Normally, he might call the police or hire more security, but he never relied on anyone when he wanted things done properly. Sandy wasn't scared. The press called him out of touch but his grandparents hadn't been rich. Sandy didn't care about the masses but he knew them and they were idiots.

Sandy drove to the site that night and surprised the night watchman who seemed relieved when Sandy wanted to check it out alone. Did he believe it was haunted too? He had come in where the bulldozers were. They were no longer tangled up, but facing each other in almost a ring.

Sandy grabbed a flashlight and a hardhat then headed into the area that would eventually be the building's lobby. It would look grand but cheaply made. His architect knew what looked rich to these young yuppies, especially the new ones who didn't have any class. Sandy had seen their McMansions that looked like someone vomited Frank Lloyd Wright. Sandy listened for signs of life, but heard nothing except the cars outside and saw nothing but the work lights that dimly lit the interior. He moved farther into the building. Still nothing. Hector was crazy or drunk or both.

Then the crying started.

He had to quiet his breathing to make sure he wasn't imagining things. He wasn't. A soft voice sobbed.

"Hello?" he called out. No response. He figured it wasn't ghosts but some homeless person crashing at the site.

When he aimed the light in the direction of the crying, a shadow passed and went into one of the unfinished doorless apartments. Sandy knew it had to be a trick of the light because the shadow almost looked transparent.

"I can see you," he said in his stern voice, the one he used on subordinates. "Better come out or I'm calling the cops. This isn't a shelter. Leave now and you won't get in trouble." Sandy lied about that. This person had fucked him over. Sandy planned to reciprocate.

The crying continued. Sandy knew he should call the cops but the idea of homeless people living in his multi-million-dollar construction site pissed him off. He moved into the empty apartment. While the crying continued, Sandy couldn't find the source. All the rooms were empty.

He knew sound could carry but the voice sounded right next to him and he had seen the shadow go into this apartment.

It started getting cold despite being seventy degrees out. Now Sandy started to get spooked. He chuckled to loosen the tension. This had to be a trick or something.

Then the screaming started. It sounded like a woman, her voice shrill, high-pitched and in pain. Sandy jumped. His arms tingled with goose bumps. Hector was a superstitious ignoramus. He couldn't have been right. Could he?

"Hello?" he said when the screaming stopped. He couldn't think of anything else to say. He didn't believe in ghosts. Maybe there was a recorder playing the screaming. Maybe a small speaker was hidden somewhere in this room. Maybe Occupy douchebags had friends who did special effects.

That was when the room filled with screaming, crying, heavy winds, and loud noises. He covered his ears and tried to find the source of the sounds, but to no avail. He could think of no explanation for such forceful winds inside the building. The sounds grew louder by the minute. Building materials flew about the room and around his face. He moved his hands to protect himself, and backed into a wall. A force grabbed him, yanked him forward about two feet, then slammed him hard against a wall.

The noises stopped.

Sandy saw nothing but blackness. In the chaos, he'd lost his flashlight. The noises and wind stopped, but now he felt a bone-chilling cold. His breath came out in fog. He didn't want to believe in ghosts—the supernatural was stuff for the stupid—but no one had been in this room and something had slammed him into the wall.

"Jesus." He rubbed his arms. Nothing seemed broken but he would have some bruises.

"What's the big deal?" he said, still only half believing. "People die in hospitals all the time. Mt. Sinai ain't ghost central."

Another loud scream filled the air. The room brightened as a flickering white light moved closer to him. Sandy got up and moved to a wall, trying to edge away from it. The thing moved closer then materialized into a shimmering African-American woman. He could see through her translucent body to the wall behind. She wore a white shirt drenched in blood and her eyes had a cold dead stare as she looked directly at Sandy. She put her hand up and pointed to the door-less entrance.

Sandy tried to stop shaking. He accepted that ghosts existed. This was not from a camera or some trick. However, mixed in with his fear was also anger. This was *his* building. He owned it; he'd bought it. It belonged to him. No one living or dead was going to drive him out.

"I'm not leaving!" he yelled. "You can't make me!"

She tried. Sandy didn't know he could fly. He felt himself rising until he reached the ceiling. This time, he started screaming.

"Let me go."

She did. He watched as the floor came hurtling towards him. When his head hit the ground, everything went dark.

He opened his eyes to a bright room. He was lying down. Not on the ground, but on a hard mattress. Nothing hurt but his body almost felt numb. Glancing around, he saw white walls. It seemed like he was in the hospital. The night watchman must have found him and called an ambulance, but why wasn't he in a room? Instead, he found himself on a gurney in the middle of a hallway. He expected doctors and nurses to come to him. He was a rich and famous real estate developer. Even if this was some city hospital, they wouldn't treat him like this. How dare they ignore him? When he looked closely, he noticed many of the other patients wore shabby clothing and most of them were black. He studied the surroundings more closely. Women wore long dresses; men wore overalls, patchwork clothes or cheap suits. The hospital was crowded. The people surrounding him were bleeding, coughing, vomiting. Suddenly, he could smell and he didn't want to. The room smelled like something he couldn't imagine and the only scent he could identify was piss.

A nurse flew by and Sandy put his arm out to flag her, but she ignored him. That was less startling than when Sandy saw his hands. Instead of white ones, they were black and small like a woman's. Then the pain came— massive, horrible, pain. Sandy turned the black hands around to see they were covered in blood. He noticed the gurney also soaked in blood. He began screaming for help from the agonizing pain, but he wasn't the only one. He could hear the sounds. Many people were screaming, begging for help. No one came to his aid.

Sandy closed his eyes. When he opened them again, he was back in the dark room lying face down on the ground. He jumped up and rubbed his arms again. He felt more pain probably from the fall, but again nothing seemed broken.

"Shit." Relief filled him. Probably for the first time, he understood being poor and was grateful he wasn't.

While the room was dark, it was still frigid. The woman was gone but he knew she was still here.

Despite the fact that Sandy was scared, bruised and battered, he wasn't about to let this building go. "Look, this happened in the past, okay, not now. Now, you would have gotten treated. There are plenty of black doctors and nurses and I heard Harlem Hospital is top notch. I want you out of my building."

The temperature dropped even further.

"Oh please," he rubbed his arms and got angrier. "Even if I died a violent and horrible death, I definitely wouldn't hang out in the place it happened. I'd haunt the Saint-Tropez or Aspen."

The room became so cold, Sandy wished for his winter jacket.

"I'm trying to be reasonable. I have a lot of money invested in this place. I'm not going to let anyone, alive or dead, take it from me. There is nothing for you here."

Sandy realized she didn't like his answer when he felt his feet come off the ground.

"Wait!" He had an idea. He knew how to grease the wheel. He kept many apartments all over the country. Places he could stay when he traveled and when he needed to get away from a girlfriend or get a quickie from a girlfriend if he happened to be married at the time. Places his friends might need to go if they wanted the same thing.

"Tell you what. How would you like to live in the lap of luxury?" There was no response but his feet touched the floor again. "This place is being turned to primo condos. Studio to three bedrooms, beautiful views, state of the art equipment and total temperature control, which I think you need. You can have an apartment for free and haunt it until the end of days if you leave the workers alone and let them finish. You also need to leave the tenants alone until they've signed. What do you say? Beautiful, sunny, three bedrooms or I leave the place like this: ugly and unfinished? 'Cause that's what I'll do. I'm a spiteful man."

The noises stopped. Sandy smiled. Even ghosts could be paid off. However, it was still freezing. She was listening but not convinced.

"Not only that, but how about a million bucks for some organization that deals with getting medical care to poor people. I mean a legitimate organization here in New York, no front. I'll make sure less poor people die. How about that? Good enough?"

The room warmed but Sandy still felt goosebumps.

"Also, I promise that a percentage of the building has some affordable housing, so lower and middle class families can buy their own apartment." Sandy was already doing the last thing; it was part of his deal with the city for evicting the previous tenants.

The room returned to the normal temperature.

"I guess that means we have a deal."

Silence. No crying, no screaming, and the place seemed empty again.

Tonight, he received some kind of award because a year ago he had donated a million dollars to a group called *People in Crisis* that guaranteed quality medical care to poor people with a promise of more gifts. He told the press he decided to do this when his assistant found out his site used to be a small urban hospital called St. Carmen. The hospital was one of the few that served the truly poor but had been mismanaged, understaffed and many of the patients had died. It had finally closed in 1890 due to negligence.

Sandy could never find out the name of the woman. Patients' names were never written down and there was almost no record of the hospital. The woman was most likely a prostitute. He didn't know why only she had remained behind to haunt it.

That wasn't his problem now. The gift had gotten him great publicity and his mystical accountant used it to get a tax write off that pretty much replaced most of the money he lost. It helped him grease the wheel and the press treated him as less of a pariah. *The Post* even talked about him running for mayor and called him the developer with heart.

The limo drove past his luxury condos on 105th Street. They finished a few months ago, and there had been no more problems with workers, no more accidents, and no more talk about El Diablo. The three low-income apartments all sold and Sandy made sure the owners were middle class African-Americans. All the other units sold for higher than market value except one: Apartment 136. Sandy kept that apartment empty, fully furnished with actual luxury items, not the fake ones he'd had installed in other apartments.

Even better was that none of the new tenants complained, nothing broke, caught fire or stopped working; they were all like a pig in shit, except those who lived in apartments 135 and 137. They wanted to know why the lady in apartment 136 was always crying.

Sandy didn't care. He only wanted to make money.

The Lost Tapes
Shane Starr
Daniel Arthur Smith

"RECORDING BEGINS WITH TODAY'S date, May 30th, 2018. My name is Agent Melissa Muldoon. Present with me is Agent Lawrence Meyer. Commencing interview of one Shane Starr. Mister Starr is the sole survivor of a Himalayan documentary expedition. I note that Mister Starr's head, hands, and feet are bandaged due to injuries from exposure. Mister Starr has established that he can hear and speak and has agreed to this interview willingly. Mister Starr, can you please state your name for the record?"

"It's…Hrrmm…It's Shane Starkowski."

"Starr isn't your legal name? I thought, with Starr Enterprises, Starr Airlines, Starr everything—"

"Starr just sounded better. It's not a secret, just not well known."

"So, I should address you as?"

"Starr is fine. But for the record, Starkowski."

"Thank you."

"Hrrmm."

"Please take your time. I understand that you are experiencing a great deal of pain."

"Oh…Okay."

"I have to tell you, Larry and I are real big fans of your show."

"That's very kind."

"I loved the episode where you tracked down those orangutans in the Borneo. Or was it Sumatra?"

"Sumatra."

"Right. Sumatra. The Bornean Orangutan is a different species than the Sumatran varieties. I remember the episode because it stuck out to me that the Bornean females don't have beards, while the Sumatrans do. But your expedition wasn't looking for the Sumatran Orangutans."

"My, you are a fan. That's right. We were in Sumatra in search of the Tapanul orangutan."

"Distinguishable by their smaller heads and flatter faces."

"I'm glad to see someone take an interest."

"More people should. To think there are only a thousand of those gentle creatures left."

"Less than that. Eight hundred."

"Only eight hundred."

"I'm very proud of the work we've done with the Adventure EveryWhere Foundation, not just the documentaries but because of the work that continues behind the scenes. Over the years, we've managed to document some of the rarest species on the planet. Seek them out…hrum…identify the threats—environmental and external. Then we do what we can to protect them. That's what we do…did."

"Did?"

"I said that's what we 'do.' But it's 'did.' That's what we 'did.' I was the only one to make it out of that camp. Ransone and the others, they weren't as fortunate."

"Yes. That's why we're here. Actually, by your request. We rarely travel outside the country, much less to Bhutan. You must have some amazing access."

"Being a billionaire has its privileges."

"I'm sure it does. What I'm confused about is why you asked for us by name."

"I've been following the work you and your partner do. You'll be interested in what I'm about to tell you. You investigate such things."

"I'm flattered and surprised that you're even aware of us. What we do is supposed to be discreet and confidential."

"As you said, I have some amazing access."

"Fair enough. What is it that you wanted to share with us? We're all ears."

"First, you have to understand that what I'm about to tell you may sound outlandish—the words of a man who has lost his mind—but I assure you…hrrmm…that it's the truth."

"Okay. I admit that I'm intrigued. Can you start from the beginning?"

"Certainly…Hrrmm…If you could help me with a drink. Would you mind?"

"Yes. Of course. Let me just maneuver the straw…There you go."

"Thank you. That's much better. Now, where was I?"

"You weren't anywhere quite yet. You were just about to start from the beginning."

"So I was. Ransone and I began planning for this expedition almost three years ago."

"You mentioned Ransone before. I remember seeing him on the show."

"He was my top man. We did the research together, but logistics belonged to him. No small job either. He arranged the permits, the transportation, lodging, the army of Sherpas we needed for the expedition and all the food to feed them, everything really."

"So many moving parts. It sounds like a grand undertaking."

"I assure you it was. The expedition routed through the Sacred Himalayan Landscape which spans across the eastern slope of the Himalayan range through three countries, each one with a separate list of requirements. But it was worth it. We were putting together material for three Adventure EveryWhere documentary specials."

"What were the three?"

"Along the way we documented the red panda and the snow leopard, but our goal was far more noble—one of the rarest animals on the face of the planet."

"Don't tell me—"

"Yes. We set out to film the Tibetan blue bear."

"The blue bear? That's not what I thought you were going to say. Has anyone ever seen a live specimen?"

"No one from the west. We were about to be the first."

"Exciting."

"But in our search, we encountered a far rarer creature."

"There it is."

"The yeti."

"You saw Bigfoot?"

"Again, a different species. Though I'm sure closely related."

"That's—"

"Unbelievable. I know. But I told you, I'm telling the truth."

"Mister Starr, do you mind if I check your chart?"

"You're a doctor?"

"No. But I've done enough forensics to learn how to read a doctor's handwriting."

"Go right ahead."

"Let's see. Three broken ribs, a broken wrist—on each hand, multiple fractures including two fractured vertebrae. But nothing in here about a concussion."

"I know what I saw."

"Mister Starr. With all due respect—"

"With all due respect, I'm telling you what I saw."

"Okay. Go on."

"The first weeks of the expedition went well. Things were running like clockwork. Ransone was extremely good at his job. The first creature we sought out was the red panda and we found it straight away. The snow leopard proved to be far more elusive. We tracked one across the Himalayan wilderness. It was on the twenty-third day that we had our first encounter. While Ransone and I scouted for a campsite, we heard some odd howling sounds which our Sherpa guide attributed to the mating calls of the snow leopard. We were elated to have finally closed in. But as the howling persisted into the night, other Sherpa became agitated. They didn't believe the cry to be coming from a leopard, and whispers of *metoh-kangmi* began to circle the fires."

"Metoh-kangmi?"

"Metoh translates as man-bear and Kang-mi as snowman."

"The man-bear-snowman?"

"That's what they said. We thought it was foolish, of course. But later that night, Lars—one of the cameramen—saw a dark shape moving across a field not far from the camp. The next morning, we discovered human-like footprints in the snow where the figure had been sighted. Over the next few days, we found more tracks, equipment tampered with, cameras tampered with. I suspected that, whatever it was, it was in search of food. Then we discovered the mutilated carcass of the snow leopard we'd been tracking."

"And the Sherpa believed this was—"

"I know, I know, ridiculous. But it didn't help that the odd howls persisted after the death of the snow leopard. These are a stalwart people of firm tradition and belief. Once the seed was planted, the course was set. Each morning, there were fewer Sherpa. Others began to say the expedition was cursed, which in turn only fueled more desertions."

"Did you discuss folding? Abandoning the expedition?"

"We did. As soon as we began to suffer attrition. It was Ransone, not me, who wanted to stay. He was concerned of the expense but mostly, I know, he didn't want to quit over such nonsense. He'd put a lot of planning into the expedition and wanted to see it through. He assured me that these things always ran their course. But he couldn't have foreseen what was to happen next."

"And what was that?"

"Our food supplies became contaminated."

"Something got into the food?"

"A storm front had moved in, so the cook made a large pot of yak milk and mushroom stew. Everyone who ate it became ill, and that was most everyone in camp."

"And you? You were ill too?"

"No. As luck would have it, I hadn't eaten that night. I'd already been suffering from a bug that was going around camp and couldn't keep anything down. But that was the last straw. I told Ransone right then that we were folding—despite the cost. He was reluctant but he had to agree. We had no idea if the food poisoning was an accident or the result of the food being tampered with, and that meant that—apart from the small amount of tins—we couldn't trust the food we had in reserve. So it was decided. As soon as the storm passed, we would evacuate."

"But you didn't evacuate."

"We never had the chance. It came that night."

"It? The yeti?"

"The storm was far fiercer then we'd anticipated. It was too dangerous to leave or even stray far from camp. You can't imagine what it's like to be in the midst of a Himalayan storm. The roar was thunderous and constant. The gales came through with the blast of a freight train, snapping treetops and blowing down the tents on the perimeter. There were a few of us that weren't sick from the food, but we still didn't have the manpower to do rapid repair. We brought the yaks into the main tent and huddled together around the stove, while those who were ill lay on the tables and benches, wherever they could, and let me tell you, the tent was foul, rancid with the odor of vomit and diarrhea so thick, we stuffed garlic into our noses and wrapped our heads with scarves. Hours into the storm, we were in dire need of fresh air, so when a lull finally came and the wind died down enough for us to think, those of us that could went to get blankets and pans for our makeshift hospital. It was while we were gathering supplies that we heard the blood-curdling banshee scream of the yeti."

"You knew it was the yeti?"

"A Sherpa spotted the silhouette against the tree line. Through the night vision binoculars, I viewed a bipedal, ape-like creature approaching the camp. The creature's head was squarish, ears close to the skull, and its shoulders sloped sharply down to a massive chest. Its body was covered with long hair, except the face and chest, and reminiscent of an orangutan but twice the size—I put it at three meters high and easily three-hundred kilograms, and as it approached, it emitted a loud, high-pitched cry."

"And you just stood there?"

"We followed the same protocol we would with any primate and froze in place as it approached, believing it wouldn't charge. We've seen this behavior countless times and didn't consider the threat too severe. We were wrong. But by time we realized that, it was too late. The men and I made a feeble attempt to fend it off. It threw us like rag dolls, tearing limbs from their sockets. I remember one of the Sherpa flying toward me. I was knocked out—I don't know if it was for seconds or minutes—but I awoke to the screams of those in the main tent."

"What did you do?"

"There are rare moments in your life when your body overrides your mind with flaring primal signals, split seconds when your heart pounds into your throat and you're frozen between breathes. When you're struck with epiphany and the complex is reduced to an instant clarity. This was one of those times. I don't remember thinking. I remember running."

"You ran from the camp?"

"I ran to my own tent, grabbed a rifle and the flare gun, then fled into the wilderness where I hid for the rest of the night. I didn't go back until morning."

"And what did you find?"

"Utter destruction. The camp was torn apart. What the storm hadn't destroyed, the beast did. The yellow tarpaulin of the main tent was maroon with dried blood, as was the surrounding snow. Arms, legs, heads were strewn about, as were intestines and organs."

"No one survived?"

"There was not a single body left whole. The yeti killed everyone but me."

"I see. You weren't found at the camp."

"No. While I was searching for survivors, I heard the howl of the yeti from the direction I'd come. It was tracking me. So I grabbed some tins and a hiking pack and fled again…and the yeti followed. It pursued me for three days and nights."

"Did it finally give up?"

"Yes, or so I thought. After a day passed without me hearing its howl, I'd thought I lost it. Every pack has an emergency beacon sewn into it, designed to be found from camp. I went to high ground to increase the range and hid on a ledge overlooking the valley. Hours passed and all was quiet. There were still no signs of rescue, but also no more of that high-pitched howling. I thought I was safe, but then the creature came out of nowhere. He had me cornered and I thought I was doomed, but I again escaped its clutches, this time by leaping from the cliff, down into the valley below. The fall would have killed me. Luckily, I landed in the boughs of a tall tree. I bounced around a bit between the branches before I dropped through and onto the forest floor."

"That would explain the three broken ribs, your broken wrists, the crushed vertebrae."

"It wasn't a soft fall. Fortunately, the emergency beacon did its job. I woke up here, then reached out to you."

"Mister Starr, we appreciate that. We really do. It's not every day we get to meet a man such as yourself. And we sympathize with the fate of your crew. But with all due respect, many people in your state have what are essentially false memories. Most likely what you saw was the blue bear you'd been tracking."

"I know what survivor shock is. And I'm not so arrogant to believe I'm above it. But this wasn't a bear."

"You're telling me your party was attacked by a giant white ape."

"No. The night vision is monochrome. I couldn't make out the color until it was close. The body fur was reddish-brown in color."

"Well...So it was a giant orangutan."

"I believe it was a species thought to be extinct, gigantopithecus blacki. But they're not extinct. I was face to face with it."

"Gigantopithecus blacki?"

"I believe it's the same species as the fossil record."

"That's amazing if true. But you have no proof."

"Ah, but you see Agent Muldoon, I do have proof. I have video. We filmed it as it approached camp. We even captured the first images of the rampage. I have the images, and I want to give them to you."

"But if you have the footage, why not release it? You'd make history, add insights to evolution, biology, the world of science."

"I told you. The work we've done with the Adventure EveryWhere Foundation is not just about the documentaries. Our mission is to seek out the rarest animals, identify the threats—environmental and external. Then do what we can to protect them. If this tape got out, the outcome for this creature would be just the opposite. Corporations, scientists, and eco-tourists would flood the habitat. We'd be responsible for its true extinction. No. I want it with you, where it will be safe. I want to partner with your agency in protecting these creatures."

"Don't worry, Mister Starkowski, you called the right people. We're in the business of being discreet."

Tales from the Canyons of the Damned

ABOUT THE AUTHORS

Michael Ezell A former US Marine and police officer, Michael now resides in Southern California with his wife, two sons, and at least five too many rescue cats.

His work has appeared in numerous anthology collections including*Tales from the Canyons of the Damned, On Spec Magazine* ,Orson Scott Card's *Intergalactic Medicine Show*, Baen Books *The Year's Best Military and Adventure SF Vol. 3*, and *Once Upon a Time in Gravity City*.

His secret identity is that of a project coordinator in the Special Makeup Effects industry. (for an Emmy-winning shop!).

Jeremy Essex is a software developer from Suffolk, England. His e-book *The Sound Of Time* is a ghostly account of paranormal events in a South Devon office building. He the author of multiple short stories, including *The Death Pool*, featured in *Kzine* issue 19, *The Phantom Of Higham Corner*, from the anthology *9 Tales Told In The Dark*, and *Aberration*, featured in *Acidic Fiction* online magazine.

M. Regan has been writing in various capacities for over a decade, with credits ranging from localization work to scholarly reviews, advice columns to short stories. Particularly fascinated by those fears and maladies personified by monsters, she enjoys composing dark fiction and studying supernatural creatures.

Lara Frater published a non-fiction book *Fat Chicks Rule! How to Survive a Thin Centric World*. It was a guidebook on being a big girl in a thin world and included information on how to fat positive books, movies, and TV, where to find fashion, comfortable seating, and how to deal with fat hatred. A few months after the book was published, I did a companion blog with the same name that she still updates every Monday.

She has published essays, poetry and short stories.

In 2012, she published *End of the Line* the first in the series of three zombie novels that take place in a world almost dead of the flu and having to deal the zombies who rose from the ashes. *End of the Line* was followed by *Stuck in the Middle* in 2013 and *Full Circle* in 2014.

She is also working on a three book dystopian series called *Welcome to Pluto*. I hope to have the first book out in 2016.

She lives in New York City with her husband, author Jonathan Frater and has lots of animals and people in her house.

Jessica West (a.k.a. West1Jess) is currently pursuing a state of self-induced psychosis, also known as writing. In the past, she has worked for Wal-Mart, a lawyer, and a bank. Now if she could just get a couple years experience with the IRS and the NSA, world domination is in the bag.

Jess lives in Acadiana with three daughters still young enough to think she's cool and a husband who knows better but likes her anyway.

For news and updates visit west1jess.com

Daniel Arthur Smith is a USA Today bestselling author. His titles include *Spectral Shift*, *Hugh Howey Lives, The Cathari Treasure, The Somali Deception*, and a few other novels and short stories. He also curates the phenomenal short fiction series *Tales from the Canyons of the Damned* and *Frontiers of Speculative Fiction.*

He was raised in Michigan and graduated from Western Michigan University where he studied philosophy, with focus on cognitive science, meta-physics, and comparative religion. He began his career as a bartender, barista, poetry house proprietor, teacher, and then became a technologist and futurist for the Fortune 100 across the Americas and Europe.

Daniel has traveled to over 300 cities in 22 countries, residing in Los Angeles, Kalamazoo, Prague, Crete, and now writes in Manhattan where he lives with his wife and young sons.

For news and updates visit danielarthursmith.com